From The Editor'

Art is conceived and received in a context. intensively reading submissions for this issu sadness, and depression at watching dark events unfold in my country. I viewed these events through my ubiquitous newsfeed, but also through a personal lens. A college student whose summer science research job got cancelled, a woman near to retirement cruelly fired, and another woman afraid to go to the store due to the color of her skin. Some of the writing in this issue speaks directly to this anger and the associated issues. You'll see the ravages of war, the consequences of forever incarceration, and long tentacles of colonialism. Other pieces of writing do what literature can do best, remove us from our day-to-day surroundings and concerns. You'll feel the glimmer of Lake Michigan, the beauty of a monsoon rain, and the nostalgia of an elementary school hallway. And a young poet gives us permission to feel joy in these times with the remarkable line: "Tell me how delight is not resistance."

Curating this issue on the occasion of Stanchion's fifth anniversary was a huge honor. Jeff has produced a gorgeous journal with kindness and integrity. Submissions came in droves and from all parts of the globe. The contributors to this issue span five continents. Please know that it was painful to decline so many wonderful pieces of writing from such diverse perspectives. As you read this issue, appreciate what Jeff has done to create such a broad literary hub and encourage others to support this endeavor.

This issue was curated with a healthy does of anger, but with a much larger dose of love. Enjoy the journey within these pages.

– François

StanchionZine.com

Edited by François Bereaud

Cover photograph by Jeff Bogle

Print ISBN: 979-8-89692-797-6

Stanchion Issue 19 Table of Contents

HEVEL

One figure towered above the rest of the leather-clad, badass women. Her long black curls gleamed in the sunlight, streaks of iron gray picking up the same glint in steely eyes. Everywhere that bare skin showed, and there were miles of it, rippled in cords like nautical rope and danced with the chains at her waist and heels.

Laurel.

A dozen of these rallies, now, and I finally had her name. It didn't matter, though. She was the enemy.

Her group wore matching vests sporting club insignia, and they stayed in tight formation. A raging tide, but with a sway that softened their swagger. Any minute they might break into Tharpian choreography, heavy boots stomping in syncopation, disrupting the heartbeat of every mammal in the vast parking lot.

Each of them hoisted a sign, some sporting skulls and dripping blood, others displaying catchy slogans, artistically scrawled.

"A helmet on your head keeps you out of a hospital bed."

Definitely not true.

"Protect your head or end up dead."

Possibly true.

"Be cool, wear your helmet."

Absolute bullshit in any sense of the word "cool." Doesn't rhyme either.

We were no slouches in the slogan department on our side, preferring to stick with the classics like, "Ride free or die."

Clubs and groups protested for both sentiments and it all became meaningless. They'd all lost someone. They were here fighting for that person. Or that's what they believed. You could see it in the lines etched around sensual mouths, the haunting depth in black-lined eyes and the determined set of firm chins. You felt it in the battle-ready stance of rounded hips.

A "Mothers Against Drunk Drivers" vibe, but more "Biker Babes Against Freedom."

Laurel's damage was hidden, yet on display. Hell, I might wear a helmet if she'd tell me her story.

She slipped through the group, greeting everyone like long-lost friends, squeezing arms, looking deeply into eyes. A succubus, pulling out the pain.

I wanted her to pull mine. I wanted it to *mean something*.

When she leaned to hug someone, my arms itched. Her intimate smile made my own lips twitch. Parading around on those legs, rocking a bit with each heavy step, she made my brain seize like a Harley on a cold morning. Tight jeans hung low, a thin stretch of flat belly showing between the cropped shirt and the heavy silver belt buckle. The tantalizing tip of an unknown tattoo crept up from her right hip. I wanted to trace it with a finger.

This would be the last one of these events. Her side was going to win. Helmet laws–the ultimate nanny state triumph. I wanted to explain it, to hold her shoulders, look in her eyes and say, "Look, Laurel, I'm sorry your friend is dead, but some things are worse than dying."

But what would be the point? My bubbie, my grandmother, once told me about hevel. The bible said everything is meaningless. She was old and wise by then, but I'd been young and impatient. I knew there must be meaning. When there isn't, we make it up, paint it on.

We have walking wounded on our side, too, they just don't come to rallies. No one wants to hear about the ones who linger. In a bed, in a coma. Their families sit beside them, eyes cried out, lives disassembled, frozen in time. Absent. Plastering meaning like a cast on a broken arm.

I remember the long hours, the quiet wait for death.

Having to choose it for someone. Arguing the decision.

I'd rather die than be planted in the hospital garden.

And it should be up to me.

I'd shouted it across steaming stretches of asphalt. Cried out to anyone, to everyone. No one listened. No one until Laurel.

Her head had tilted while her soft eyes searched me. Why did I fight, she wanted to know. We'd stared at each other for the longest time.

I wondered if she ever thought about that moment. I also wondered if she had a tattoo on her other hip. Maybe lower, so it didn't show.

When that crowd looked at us, they saw lawless wild things, determined to have the wind in our hair. As if feeling a breeze were the most important thing in life.

Maybe it should be.

We were a small group on my side. Fighting to apply dignity to an utterly undignified life. Mostly, our people were the tiny intersection of those who ride and also work in hospitals. We want to decide the outcome for ourselves, before someone does it at a beeping display panel.

We were going to lose this battle, but I had lost my will to fight anyway. Long after she tried to tell me, long after she was gone, I wanted to tell Bubbie she'd been right. Nothing mattered. But their win gave these broken humans something they needed. It gave Laurel something, and I wanted her to have it.

I smoothed my hair, dusted my jacket, and patted my backside. My own jeans were flatteringly snug, too. I marched over. Fraternizing with the enemy? Would my co-workers see? Would they care? I couldn't let this end and never see her again, never learn her story. Somehow, she'd become my last hope of proving my grandmother wrong.

"Hi. Um, Laurel?" Not my best opening. She half-turned. Unfortunately, when she did, I found myself up close with those storm-cloud eyes. A shock of thick lashes framed them, capturing me like tiny prison bars.

"Yes? Oh, hi. How are you?" She smiled politely. The dimples emerged and I was done in. Done for. Just done.

"I'm, um, I'm great thanks. Listen, congratulations."

At that, she turned all the way toward me studying my face to see if I mocked her. Music blared out of giant speakers and I had to lean close. I could feel her body heat, smell leather and lavender.

"Y-you all fought hard for the win, here," I stammered.

"Thanks," she said. "We did."

Vindication. Was that a type of meaning?

I wanted to ask. I looked at the others, their tragedies etched on their faces.

"So," I sputtered, regaining her attention. "Since I won't see you at any more of these…" Deep breath, plunge onward. "I was wondering, would you like to get together sometime? I mean, without any protesting?"

That didn't come out quite like I intended. Those glorious silver orbs narrowed to speculative slits and swept me from head to toe, then locked in, eye to eye.

"I think I'd like that." She reached behind to pull her phone out of her back pocket, the move as lithe as a dance. "What's your number?"

The buzz in my pocket let me know she'd gotten it right.

"Thanks, I'll call you." I turned away, then swung back and added, "Soon."

"Okay." Her bright smile was triumphant, but gracious. I felt a little triumphant myself.

"Hey," she called over the noise as I walked away. "This is better. You'll see."

My smile was less enthusiastic.

The overlapping growl of many bikes revving snaked up my spine. That and the music from the loudspeaker enveloped me in an oblivious cocoon, daydreaming about getting to know Laurel. When the music changed to a catchy rap song, my stroll adjusted to the rhythm, cruising to the beat.

My friends were all staring at me, horror on their faces. They couldn't be that upset that I crossed the enemy line, could they? But they weren't staring at me, they were staring past me. I turned slowly to look, bracing myself for whatever they'd seen.

I could never have prepared myself. Highly polished chrome glinted in the late afternoon sun, where it wasn't trapped under the glossy black sports car. Neither moved. No one moved. The world stood still.

My feet changed direction, and my walk became a run. When I could see through the gathering crowd, I slowed.

Black curls spilled out from a full-face helmet and the long jeans-clad legs stuck out behind a tire. Another inch of that tattoo was revealed but it floated in a spreading crimson lake of blood and reeking gasoline.

I couldn't see the other hip.

Did it, too, carry a mark? I knew little about Laurel and I would never know more.

Hevel.

Aaron Menzel

BOTCHED

"You gotta whack her on the neck. See? Here. That's called the *jugular*." Scoutmaster Quintin traced an "X" across the feathers as the bird tried to wiggle free. "And it's gotta be quick. One hit. Just like Paul did. Then take her to the blood bucket."

"Her?" I said.

"Yuh-huh. She's a hen."

"I'm killing a girl?"

"You're killing a chicken."

"A girl chicken."

"A hen."

"A child. A baby. I'm calling her 'Henrietta'."

"Aaron," Scoutmaster Quintin said, slowly, like he always does when he's talking to me, like, if he doesn't talk slowly everything will spill too quickly and make a mess. "It's not going back in the cage. You're the only one left. You watched Thomas and Nick. You know how it works. Now harvest and get to plucking."

He placed Henrietta on the stump, making sure to fit her neck between the gap in the two nails pegged in the center of the circle of pine. Her scaly feet dangled over the edge of the stump and the other scouts watched me from the campfire. Their chickens cooked in the stockpot bubbling over the coals. Henrietta squirmed against the wood, but Scoutmaster Quintin held the body in place and handed me the hatchet.

I took it. It was heavy, like the baseball bat from when I played for the YMCA. I remember that my swings never connected until Coach let

8

me hit off a tee. And even then I hacked at the ball from the bottom until it popped up for the pitcher to catch. And everyone laughed. Even Coach.

"I don't think I'm hungry and--"

"Doesn't matter."

"But it's kinda cruel."

"Aaron. Your folks signed the slip. Now buck up. You ain't in Girl Scouts."

I knelt by Henrietta and Scoutmaster Quintin placed my free hand on her stomach. He stretched the body back, pulling her neck tight against the nails--like a rubberband ready to snap. I raised the hatchet and swung down.

"Again!" Shouted Scoutmaster Quintin. "Again, damn it!"

On the stump, Henrietta's beak opened and closed, but no sounds came out, only blood from the gash I'd carved into her neck. I let go, and Henrietta ran.

"Get her, Aaron! Get her now!"

Henrietta tumbled toward the forest, and I ran after her. Her wings churned, and she kept zigging. My hiking boots felt heavy on my feet and I tried not to think about how parts of my face were hot and sticky from where her blood got me. Then she entered the trees.

I looked back at Scoutmaster Quintin, who screamed and waved me on, his belly hanging over his belt, the hatchet stuck into the stump. *What does it matter now? She' s gone.* But then I looked at the boys and they were all cackling.

So I ran in after her.

The forest was thick, but she was easy to follow. Blood on the fallen leaves, and I soon caught up. I slowed and got real big and put my hands out, like I'd seen on those animal shows, but Henrietta didn't seem to know I was there, even as I stood above her.

She hopped from foot to foot. I nudged her and she turned around, her neck like the Mark McGwire bobblehead Dad bought me.

I screwed up.

I could see bits of flesh and bone peeking out from under the feathers, and her beak had stopped moving. Her eyes had gone gray and even though her feet scratched at the dirt, she didn't go anywhere. From the clearing came the sound of Scoutmaster Quintin, still screaming, and the scouts, still howling away, but in the forest, it was pretty quiet. Breeze. Branches. Birdsong here and there. And if I'm telling the truth, it was probably the best part of the camping trip so far. Just the silence. Nobody screamin'. Nobody fartin' on my pillow or unstaking my tent in the moonlight. Just me and the trees and Henrietta. All on the same team.

I hunkered down and reached out for Henrietta. She shoulda been dead, but she wasn't. She was a mistake I needed to fix. Before I could think too much, I breathed in and pinched her head between my fingers and gave a little tug. Nothing. I tugged again and this time she rose into the air, so I put my hand on her back. Her feathers were soaked with blood, but when I gave another yank and her head popped off, only a little liquid bubbled up. Guess she'd run out.

"I broke you," I whispered as the leaves whispered back *shhhhhhh*. "And I can't put you back together. I've never been good at puzzles."

I cradled her head as I scraped a grave in the mud. The body went in first. I put her head on the downy feathers of her belly before scooping dirt and twigs over top. Nothing fancy, but better than her cage, I suppose.

Back at the campsite, I overheard Scoutmaster Quintin talking to Thomas about how good his chicken tasted. He said Thomas had done right by the chicken. That when a creature experiences stressful situations, a chemical called 'adrenaline' goes into the blood. That can make the muscles tense up, making meat no good, stringy, worthless.

He looked at me.

I don't think he was talking about Henrietta.

PHOTOGRAPH BY JEFF BOGLE

nat raum

SELF-PORTRAIT AS BALTIMORE

because listen, i have been vilified
too long for everything i am and also
everything i'm not. i am a creature
of habit, papas bravas or cheesy tots
or any other number of meals
which have retired from the city
but live forever in the memory
of my taste buds. i am chronically
all talk and impulsive actions.
of course i went to the charles
to get my copy of the *beat* tonight
and of course i went to tapas after
and of course i drove home with bass
from "walla walla" rattling my civic
because i can only stand noise
when i am its originator. i have never
existed as neatly in any block of baltimore
as now, blurry memories of midtown
ligatured with southeast scenes, the kind
of cinematic crispness i once looked too
closely at, thought *surely this cannot*
be real. i have never felt this energy
outside the city—it simmers down
eutaw street to just above camden
yards and hangs a left. it dissipates

in garden suburbs that wouldn't claim
us, goblins and rats of the night
scavenging for new parts of ourselves,
personality traits. my therapist says
we have a particular survivalism here—
it is not lost on me, the comparison.

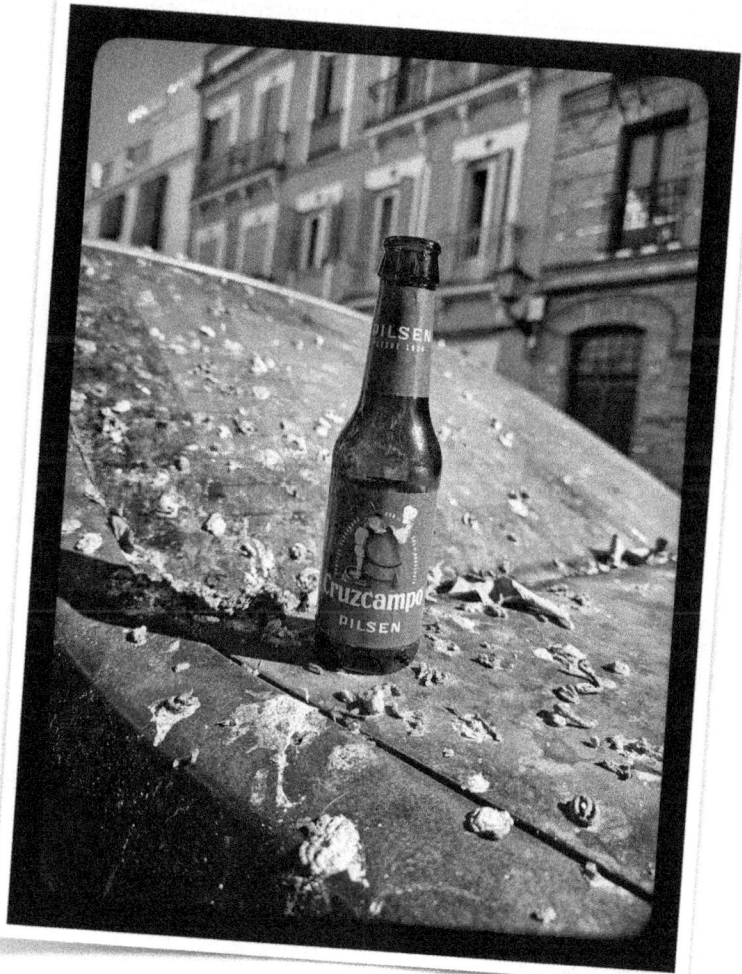

PHOTOGRAPH BY JEFF BOGLE

Sudha Balagopal

THE ARITHMETIC OF MARRIAGE

Addition

    At age ten, you're wedded to twenty-one year-old mathematics genius Srinivasa Ramanujan, but must wait three more years before you can move into his home. You don't comprehend everything marriage entails, but soon realize you must share him with his other great love, numbers.

Subtraction

    You're fifteen when he departs India for England in 1914—to pursue higher studies. Sorrowful because he says you're too young to accompany him, you imagine him in the foreign land, head brimming with theorems and equations, freezing in unfamiliar climate, struggling as a vegetarian, a lone brown man among white people—all this during war time. Anxious, you send missive after missive, receive no reply.

Multiplication

    He returns five years later, ill from lack of food or the cold—in time you learn it was tuberculosis—but continues his incessant calculating-solving-writing. However, your joy grows manyfold; after years, he's returned to you. What if he didn't answer your letters? You're blessed to take care of him. Then, it slices to discover your mother-in-law hid his responses from England, reasons unknown.

Division

    You're bereft when he dies the following year. The man who

knew infinity ascends to heaven and you sink into a void. You're barely twenty-two. His work will be a gift to the world of mathematics, to posterity. What's to become of you, no husband, no education, no child?

Remainders carry forward

He's gone, yet you remain. You pack your saris, travel to Bombay, where you learn English and tailoring, return home to open a sewing school. Finally, at age fifty, your heart swells with love again when you adopt a son. People criticize, as is their wont, say you're too old. You close your eyes, listen to your mathematician husband whisper, "Have I told you fifty is a fascinating number?"

PHOTOGRAPH BY JEFF BOGLE

A MILO BAUGHMAN

The first time Joe saw the chair was the first time he visited his mom at Riverside, the palliative care facility. He'd left Brooklyn after his shift at the bar, drove seven-plus hours, and arrived in Maine exhausted. In his late fifties, he was no longer the Superman of his youth. Gone were the days of being picked up outside the bar at closing time, with a pocket full of cash, and driving with a car full of drinking buddies to Atlantic City, where they'd gamble and run the cocktail waitress ragged till noon the next day. On the way home, he'd nap in the back seat, and they'd drop him off at the bar, just in time to bathe in the sink and start a shift that would end at two or four the next morning. That was a different person.

His stomach was buzzing from the combination of exhaustion, caffeine, a sleeve of Oreos, and anxiety. In the past twenty plus years he'd driven this route at least fifty times and had found that driving at night, when the traffic was nonexistent, loading up on podcasts, and taking a break for a good meal were the keys to making the trip and remaining sane, but this time, he just wanted to get there as fast as possible.

As he pulled into the parking lot, he was relieved Riverside wasn't ugly soul-crushing new construction. He had been imagining it would look like one of those eyesore cookie-cutter chain hotels that dotted the exits on 184. But this place was old and substantial. He thought it must have started life off as somebody's turn-of-the-century mansion, or maybe built as an old age home for retired sea captains. It was an indication that maybe this whole experience wouldn't be as bad as he had been anticipating.

None of this was exactly a surprise, she'd been sick for a decade, but stable, so Joe had not been expecting her call from the hospital a few days ago. The night before she'd had trouble breathing and was feeling panicky, and she'd called an ambulance. The next morning her doctor ran a bunch of tests and told her what they both knew was coming, that her organs were starting to fail. That meant she was dying, maybe slowly, maybe not. Hard to say. After more tests and consultations, it was determined that there was nothing they could do for her at the hospital, and arrangements were made for her transfer to Riverside.

When Joe first entered the room, his mom was asleep. She looked like herself, but pale and as if time had caught up with her. She had always looked younger than her age, and since Joe's last visit that gap had closed, and it was a bit shocking to see. The room was small but cozy and the old wood floors, ancient never-painted molding, and high ceilings were charming and distinctly un-hospital-like, and Riverside was true to its name, there was a view of the Kennebec River that boarded the leaf-covered lawn and parking lot from the window. There was a 1970s industrial Formica end table next to the bed and on it, a newspaper opened to the crossword puzzle, which was a relief to Joe – a signal his mom was still engaging in some aspects of regular life. But as he stood there and surveyed the room, alone with his thoughts, waiting for his mother to wake up, what caught Joe's attention most was the chair next to the bed. He was no furniture expert but knew this was an example of mid-century modern design. His immediate thought was "This is a perfect object." It was a low armchair with curved wooden arms the color of amber or dark honey and simple but elegant rectangular cushions that were a rusty shade of orange. The chair managed to be refined but also had a sense of fun to it. He imagined an Apollo astronaut sitting in the chair, smoking a pipe and watching a ball game. Then his mom opened her eyes and said "Joe?" A bit more life came back into her face. "Sit down," she said.

Joe scooted the chair closer to the bed and sat down. He took his mother's hand, and she slowly, but with humor, recounted the events of the last few days. She was not a complainer. Joe used to say semi-jokingly that she was "Compulsively glass half full." She'd get served the wrong entrée at a restaurant and eat it anyway, or get hopelessly lost because someone gave her the wrong address and claim it was some sort of blessing in disguise. For years, decades really, this had driven Joe crazy. He'd spent countless hours trying to get her to admit that some event in her life where she'd been treated poorly or disrespectfully had, at least a little, bothered her, but she never budged. However, in the past few years, Joe began to wonder if it wasn't her stubborn denial of reality that was in some way keeping her alive, against all doctor's predictions. As she talked, he was thinking about all of this, and how much he would miss her, but there was a part of him that was thinking about the chair, and how he might get it out of that room.

Later in the morning he drove to her house, ate some non-gas station food, and took a shower and got some sleep. This house had been his aunt's. He'd just been a kid when the aunt left Brooklyn to marry a guy from Maine and the whole thing seemed mysterious at the time. He'd imagined the aunt moving to "Main," and on his first visit as a kid was surprised to find it less developed than Brooklyn. After both sisters' husbands died young, Joe's mother happily accepted the invitation to move into the big house, selling her Brooklyn townhouse for thirty times what they'd bought it for. A few years later the sister died, and Joe wondered if his mom would want to move back to New York, but she stayed put.

Looking around there was a lot to do. Some yard work, small repairs to make, getting the house ready for the coming winter, and in the very back of his mind - eventually to sell. He opened a drawer in the kitchen looking for a pencil and found an archive of fascinating ephemera. Matchbooks to long closed night clubs, a roll of undeveloped Instamatic film, a sheet of S&H green stamps, a men's watch with a glow-in-the-dark dial – but no pencil.

That afternoon he went back to Riverside and spent most of the visit watching his mother sleep. She just couldn't help nodding off, and when she did wake, she'd apologize for not being a good host. Joe was taken with how comfortable the chair was, he could sit in it for hours without getting restless, the cushions firm but soft. Joe examined the chair more closely, looking for a tag or something to identify its origin. There was a part of him that thought he must be wrong, that this was some modern piece of disposable garbage from Ikea or Target that you buy in a box and assemble with an included allen wrench, but this thing was solid and must have been made by craftsmen. He was photographing the chair when his mom woke up and said "What are you doin' Joey?" He was struggling for an answer when she fell back asleep.

Joe had brought an old photo album he unearthed from the house, and when his mom had the energy, they looked through it together. In every photo, she was stunning. He wished he'd had a chance to know the younger radiant version of her. They laughed at her fashion choices from the sixties and seventies. There were some wild prints, bright colors and wide bell bottoms that almost seemed like outfits for a costume party, but she pulled the looks off confidently and Joe was filled with love for her unconventional spirit. His mom had worked for years decorating windows in Manhattan department stores and through that community had made friends with a bit more of a creative bent than most of their neighbors in Windsor Terrace. She had a saying "Aesthetics matter," and as a kid, Joe learned that if you needed to spend a little extra time comparing objects in a shop, it was not a waste of time, because aesthetics mattered. It offended her if a store had a sloppy handwritten "No CHANGE for the BUS" sign attached to the door with too much peeling scotch tape, because aesthetics mattered. "BATHROOM FOR CUSTOMERS ONLY!!!" was another one that drove her nuts. "The world is ugly enough," she used to say. She introduced the ideas of style and taste to Joe at a young age. From her he learned the fine line of caring enough to make things look good but never veering into vanity or pretentiousness. He wondered how she'd feel about him stealing the chair. Occasionally, she used to come home with clothes for Joe that had been used in a Macy's window display and she was always quick to point out that they had been given to her, but he was never sure if that was a hundred percent true. He wished she could weigh in and help him decide or that they could share in the planning of the chair's removal. He thought she might get a kick out plotting the heist, it would be their secret, one last adventure. But he knew it would only be a burden. What would he say? "Hey Mom, do you think I should steal this chair... from the room you're eventually going to die in?" No.

Joe got to know the doctors and the nurses and brought a box of donuts for them on most visits which elevated Joe to superstar visitor status. He quickly learned which of the staff were useless shirkers, and which could get things done and provide answers. His favorite was a nurse named Kristen who seemed to do twice as much work as anyone else. Joe was grateful that she answered his questions with no hedging, and it was Kristen who told Joe that his mom might be in more pain than she was letting on, something that the doctors hadn't caught. His mom admitted that some stronger pain relief meds might be nice, and they hooked a morphine drip into her IV, which made her sleep even more. One afternoon Kristen walked into the room and saw Joe using a tape measure and writing down the chair's dimensions. It could have been awkward, but Kristen just said "That's a nice chair, right?" and then switched the conversation to how Joe was feeling, and asking about what Brooklyn was like.

One afternoon Joe took a wander around The Riverside. The night before he'd been lying awake in bed going over scenarios for getting the chair out of his mom's room and it occurred to him that maybe his chair wasn't the only one. Maybe there was another one closer to one of the fire exit doors, or one that wouldn't have to be carried down a hundred feet of hallway and two flights of stairs or lowered out the window after sneaking forty feet up rope up to his mom's room. He checked every floor, and every unlocked door, but there wasn't another mid-century piece in the whole building. He wished he knew the chair's story. How did it wind up there?

That evening Joe drove up to an antiques mall in Wiscasset. Maybe he could just buy a similar chair, or at least find out what the chair was worth. It was a cavernous place, well organized with enough interesting things to start a museum. A well-priced silk-screened propaganda poster from the Second World War caught Joe's eye, but he was surprised how much of the stuff for sale wasn't technically antique at all. The worst was a display of signs that were painted with phrases like "You Are Amazing" and "Dream." They were produced to look old with faux antiquing, probably in a factory a million miles from

Maine. To Joe they were the opposite of inspiring. Eventually, a salesperson found Joe and asked if he needed any help. Joe pointed to the signs and asked, "Who buys these things?" The salesman shook his head and responded, "I don't understand it, but we sell tons of those… you looking for anything in particular?" Joe showed him the photos of the chair on his phone and the salesman said, "I think this might be a Milo Baughman, but who knows." From the salesman, Joe learned that putting a price on the chair was not a simple matter. If there was a pair, they'd both be worth more, but there were thousands of similar designs, with subtle differences that made some of them much more collectible than others. He suggested Joe check eBay to see what comparable pieces had sold for, but if you put a gun to his head, he'd price it in the store for $1900, and if it didn't sell in a few months put it on sale for $1500, but take $1200 if offered. Just as Joe was leaving the store the salesman said, "But in New York or L.A., thirty-five hundred… five thousand… who knows?" Back at the house, Joe spent most of the night on his laptop reading about the history of furniture and looking at eBay where there were plenty of cool $7,000 chairs one could buy.

The next morning the doctor confirmed it was Joe's mom's kidneys that were failing, and he took Joe aside and told him she probably had "Three, maybe four five days." Joe spent much of that day sitting in the chair, talking to his mom when she was awake about whatever came into his mind. His work, his girlfriend, his ex-wife, the old neighborhood, vacation plans. They both knew what was happening, but never mentioned it directly. She told him things that would be helpful later, like where the folder was where she kept warranties, and what realtor in town she trusted. Joe had brought a few things from the house to make the room feel more familiar. A few framed photos, a crochet blanket, and a favorite vase she'd received as a wedding present. The vase looked like a tangle of bamboo and Joe set it on the side table. Kristen came in to check on things pointed to the vase and said, "That's a stunner. Can I get some flowers for it?" She added that the nurse's station was always filled with flowers and Joe realized patients probably died in this place every day, and that the flowers were from their rooms. Kristen took the vase and brought it back with a fresh bouquet and tucked the bedding in around Joe's mom's fragile looking arms. Joe wondered if Kristen had slowly become used to working in a place where death was such a normal occurrence or were some people just more at ease with dying than he was. He made a mental note to leave the vase as a thank-you for Kristen when this was all over.

As his mom dozed his mind went back to the chair. He vacillated between planning the physical theft and ruminating over the morality of the whole crazy idea. Stealing was wrong. Joe knew that. "Would you like it if somebody stole your chair?" Joe asked himself, and the answer was a hard "No." So, why did Joe think it might be okay to steal this chair? Joe had a million answers. The corporate owners didn't value it. It needed to be appreciated. It was here by mistake and probably wasn't even owned by The Riverside. The whole medical system was a rip-off.

His mom asked for a milkshake, the first thing she'd wanted in days. One thing Joe did not understand about Maine was why the diners all closed at two pm. He was sure if you drilled down on this one fact, you'd understand the philosophical difference between the people of Brooklyn and Maine. Brooklyn people were omelets, disco fries, and cheesecake at three in the morning. Maine people were locked up at home, not hustling every second, minding their own business, happy to deny themselves and wait for breakfast. Or maybe not. Maybe it was just about population density and supply and demand, and people were the same everywhere. Joe didn't know anything anymore. He went off to their favorite diner for lunch. It was a gorgeous old place that looked frozen in time, its art deco interior only marred by the giant glowing ATM and oversized yellowing "CASH ONLY" sign. Joe felt like shouting "HEY! Aesthetics matter!" but instead he ordered lobster eggs benedict and two vanilla milkshakes to go. He had eaten there often enough over the years that the staff treated him with the casual good humor they conferred only to regulars. The waitress was a young woman in Converse hi-tops and a tee shirt that said, "The Brown" which he knew was the name of the band she was lead singer of. As she dropped the check, he asked her if she ever stole anything. Almost instantaneously she answered, "Sure, tons of shit."

Back at the hospital, he gave the other shake to Kristen who said, "You made my day!" He considered carefully breaking the chair down into sections that would fit into a duffel bag that could be smuggled out a few pieces at a time, but the chair was too well constructed, and he knew he'd just ruin it. He considered just walking out the front door with it, and if questioned, he'd just boldly lie and say the chair was his mom's. Was some receptionist making minimum wage gonna stop him? Would she even notice? And if it all went bad, he could just plead grief, and the chair would wind up back in the room. Nobody was going to jail.

Over the next couple of days, Joe had lots of time to think. While raking leaves, while showering, while back at Riverside sitting in the chair. Healthwise things were getting exponentially worse. His mom was getting more morphine, sleeping more, and talking less, almost not at all. Joe was thankful he didn't have the torment of rehashing regrets about their relationship, but there were a million things he'd do differently if he could live his life over, maybe address his gambling a bit earlier for one, but he and his mom had always understood each other and that gave him great comfort. Occasionally, Joe's mom would awake in a fairly lucid state and once she said out loud, to no one in particular, "I'm ninety-two." But what was funny is that throughout Joe's life, there'd been some suspicion about her age, stories where dates didn't line up, and documents with birth years that had been crossed out. If you had asked Joe a week before, he would have answered that his mom was eighty-eight. It was good to finally know the truth.

On the fifth morning, Joe arrived to find his mom's breathing had slowed and her skin had lost some of its pinkness and had developed a pearly translucent quality. He sensed it wouldn't be long, but part of him thought she might hang on like this for a few days. When she occasionally opened her eyes, he wasn't sure if she saw him sitting there. By the afternoon Joe was stunned by how infrequently she took a breath. It seemed like minutes would go by between exhales. Eventually, the interval between breaths had been so long that Joe knew she was gone. She had just gradually slowed down till she stopped.

After a few minutes alone Joe walked to the nurses' station and was relieved to find Kristen still on duty. He told her he thought his mother had died. There was only one nurse who was certified to legally pronounce death, and while they waited for that nurse to arrive Kristen asked Joe questions about his mom and her life. Joe had a hard time keeping it together as the first wave of understanding washed over him. He thought he had been mentally prepared, but he felt lost. Kristen snapped him out of his fog when she said one word. "Hug?" Joe was unsure. Kristen sensed this and added, "Just a short one." Joe nodded and she hugged him, and it felt good.

They told Joe to take all the time he wanted to say his goodbyes, though various staff he'd never seen before kept poking their heads in the door, and he got the idea that he should get out of their hair. He packed up her things and as he was preparing to leave the room for the last time, he took a last long look at her. She was still beautiful. He wasn't a religious person, and wouldn't describe himself as spiritual in any way, but he had an idea that what had happened had been okay, a normal part of life. It was simple. You get old, you die. It wasn't an eloquent thought, but it made sense of the whole thing to him. You die. Why would you expect anything else to happen to you?

Down in the office, there were forms to sign and a few decisions to make. The administrator's tone was soothing but practiced. As he got up to go Joe half expected the lady to say, "Please give us five stars on Google if you enjoyed your experience here."

He walked to his car and just as he was unlocking the doors he saw the chair. It was sitting at his hatchback as if it was waiting to be loaded in. He looked around and didn't see any people or a note or any clues. Then he glanced up to the window of his mom's room, and there was Kristen putting fresh linens on the bed. She turned to close the blinds, and their eyes met. She gave Joe a quick wave and a tilted-head smile.

Joe admired how the wooden arms and legs of the chair glowed in the late afternoon sun and noted how the autumn colors complemented the chair's upholstery. Aesthetics mattered. He sat down, just for a few seconds, and took in the smell of the leaves and the sound of the river. He appreciated the way the chair felt against him, supporting him. Then he carefully put the chair into the back of the car. He wasn't sure what to do next.

PHOTOGRAPH BY JEFF BOGLE

Akhila Pingali

SINGLE WOMAN SEEKS AN APARTMENT DURING AN EARLY INDIAN MONSOON

"And the blue whale whose heart is the largest room / I'll never enter"
– Alina Stefanescu, "The Smallest House is a Situation"

It is something to be
on the cusp of possibility. On a street
just the right size to love me
and leave me be, this could be mine.
I could round a corner, following
a house-tree's sprawl into
the mouth of a prinia. Under the sky
now an old-construction grey
the place looks pretty as a parcel. Does it know
that rampant bougainvillea
gift-ribbons make? Do its many playing children?
One could invite me and I could grow old
in the game.

This could be mine, all of these. Sky
like a freshly mopped marble
floor behind the slate and gold-foil sun.
Wind swinging open the doors
of two rooms and a kitchen. Or I could be theirs.

Noses dimpled against windows
slide off in the rain.
I throw my voice at the ponderous
sky. I must leave here
but then I must seal
off a road.

In our trial rooms for other people's lives
you hang yours behind the door.
Those aren't the only rooms you watch yourself in.
The houses are lined up
like pastel sentinels at the gates of
propriety and at one of them
I stop to make a call.
Go up the stairs, enter a blue whale's heart.
It tells me to come back when something can be mine.
It beats loud and slow.

Elizabeth Rosen

BOY ON A CHIMNEY

When the police arrive, the boy is standing on the chimney, just as tall and still as if he were part of the building himself. His face is lifted to the horizon. His arms hang loose at his sides. Even his brown hair, curled over the tops of his ears, isn't moving in the air currents at that height.

In front of the house, firemen sit on the bumper of their fire engine, beveled hats hanging off their knees, heavy jackets unbuckled in the spring sunshine. They are waiting to hear if they should extend their long ladder up to the boy on the chimney and carefully, carefully creep out to the end to lead him down to earth again.

All day, people mill about on the street to see what will happen. The police ring the patchy yard with crime scene tape. It's not a crime to stand on a chimney, but it's the only tape they have, and the bystanders gather behind it to watch the boy on the chimney.

The negotiator encourages the boy's family to try to get him to come down. He hands his bullhorn to the boy's mother whose tearful pleas break the hearts of the bystanders. She tells the boy on the chimney about the tamales she's made him. She describes putting a dab of his favorite pork filling into the masa and then rolling and tying the husk closed. She describes the warm corn smell of the tamale steam filling the house on which he stands. Her description is so filled with love and longing that bystanders find their mouths filling with desire.

But the boy on the chimney doesn't look down, and though the negotiator refuses to give up, no amount of yelling at the boy through a bullhorn seems likely to get him to leave his perch.

After school, a bunch of kids from his school come by. They shout up greetings and questions and jokes about where he will piss when he needs to piss. When no answer is forthcoming, they begin to jeer and insult him instead, until the negotiator, worrying about the effect of this casual cruelty, shoos them away, reminding them that if they can't say something nice. The kids make rude gestures at the negotiator and slink off to the nearest Wawa to get 48-ounce sodas and bags of chips before returning to lean in the doorways across the street where they can keep an eye on the boy on the chimney.

At some point, it occurs to someone to wonder what the boy on the chimney is looking at. They want to see what he sees. The bystanders boost one of the students up into the paltry branches of a tree the city has planted along the run-down street. They encourage him to climb as high as he can and tell them what is out there. The tree is young and thin and weakened by air pollution, and even though the climber is, too, he does his best to get high in the branches. He is not nearly so high as the boy on the chimney, but he is high enough to feel the breeze above the warm tarmac of the street. High enough to peek between the limp leaves and see the city from a new angle.

When the bystanders call up, asking him what he sees, there is a moment when he considers not answering, considers what it would be like to stay up in the branches and never touch the ground again. When he shimmies down the mottled trunk to the street, he tells the crowd he doesn't know what the boy is looking at, but as soon as their attention has shifted, he slips away, making his solitary way home where he closes his bedroom door and spends the next two days writing poems about being untethered from the earth.

Intent on this task, he will not know that as the sun loses height, the negotiator and fire chief and family huddle together in consultation. He will not see the fire chief nod at his crew, or the firemen rise, stiff with sitting, to extend the ladder on their truck, up, up, until finally there is a long, gradual bridge connecting the truck to the very edge of the chimney where the boy shuffles, barely, like a sea gull being nudged along a ledge.

Nor will the boy-poet see the fireman slowly ascend the ladder, stopping several feet below the chimney and laying his forearms along the handrails of the ladder as he leans forward to speak with apparent casualness to the boy on the chimney. Nor will he see the boy on the chimney follow the fireman down, down the easy slope of the ladder, back to his mother's tamales and the stuff of silt, never - despite repeated questions through the years - to reveal why he was on the chimney at all.

The poet will not learn all this until leaving his room several days later, but thereafter, passing each other in the school hallways, the boys will recognize something in the other that knows what it is to be temporarily unmoored, and nod.

Dorothy Lune

SANDBOX

We had to burn wood
to heat up the water in the bathtubs.
We had to burn skin to feed the European architects.

There was a casualty:
a bricklayer fell from an unfinished balcony
& turned into a muted red ochre,

the snakes cleaned up his remains.

We had to carry wooden coffins
on our backs across rivers– we had to act
wooden, business casual, gray hair & gray suits–

it's all quite casual.
A sandbox is an imitation of the desert,
even after you were born on the sand, a patch of its scent

dries on the back of your neck like milk.

PHOTOGRAPH BY JEFF BOGLE

Shehrazade Zafar-Arif

THE SILENT DEAD IN THE HOWLING EARTH

The sun had no choice but to shine on the rubble of the city.

The city, which had once been a city with a name and a history. But now this was what remained: sunlit rubble.

Zahid stood surveying the wreckage of the bazaar - what had once been a bazaar - and tried his best not to conjure up an image of what it had looked like before the blast. But it came to him nonetheless, splintered fragments, splashes of colour on a canvas. The dominant colour was blue: blue pottery, the ripple of blue silk shawls, the glint of blue lapis lazuli beads in a necklace, sheets of blue cotton held up by wooden pools to cast shade over the labyrinth of stalls.

Winding alleys leading nowhere and everywhere, a marvel on every corner, the birdsong call of vendors beckoning to the sea of shoppers: *come buy, come buy.*

Even now he could hear the echo of that relentless chant: *come buy, come buy.*

Distorted.

Come die, come die.

Zahid shook his head and considered his surroundings with the clinical procession of a surgeon looking on an open body. He continued onwards. Even the sky was empty. The birds had fled in the aftermath of the explosion, and the silence that remained was eerie and thoughtless. Debris crunched under Zahid's feet, a carpet of crushed glass and shards of pottery, wispy bits of fabric and gleaming stones from broken jewellery. A wasteland of treasures, with only him to bear witness.

But he wasn't a treasure hunter. He was merely here to look for bodies.

*

Zahid hadn't volunteered right away, when the war began. Although it hadn't been a war then, just an endless rain of fire from nondescript fighter jets. Then it became a matter of bombs: exploding under cars and ambulances, ripping their way through schools and hospitals. Bombs led to bodies, bloodstains smearing the streets he had walked through to get to school what felt like a lifetime ago. People stopped being people and became... bits. Bits and pieces.

Zahid had just finished university, and was still living with his parents. Before the war, the future had been a nebulous concept, vague musings about getting a job or moving abroad to study further. After the war, the future became even fainter, little more than a possibility, the promise of life but not a guarantee of it.

He couldn't bear the hiding and the praying and the constant flinching when the bombs fell, so he decided to volunteer. His mother had wept the first time he'd walked out the door, but she didn't stop him. All around the country, thousands of mothers wept. You could fill a river with their tears. So what made her tears that much more valuable when her son, her boy, left for work wearing a bullet-proof vest and a helmet that would do little to protect him if a bomb decided to fall?

Decided to fall. As if they were sentient, thinking things, malicious creatures from outer space with the singular purpose of killing without discrimination. If only.

His mother still cried every time he left the house, and his sister whispered a prayer and blew in his direction, like a kiss. It annoyed him, because they acted as though he was off doing something heroic, like saving lives or treating the injured. But in truth, he was just a glorified gravedigger.

*

The bodies, Zahid's boss had explained to him, were important. People needed something to bury, or they would forever fret that their loved one hadn't made the safe passage to heaven - or worse, that they were still alive, and wandering dazed and disoriented through the rubble. That hope could kill you faster than a well-timed bomb.

So Zahid and his crew searched for proof of death, fishing out dusty corpses from underneath the debris, digging them out of the dirt only to bury them again. Sometimes all they could find and retrieve was a severed limb. But people had taken to writing their names on their arms and legs and torsos, so that if only a piece of them was found, it could be identified, processed, and sent home. Sometimes they got lucky and found multiple pieces, which they were then able to assemble into something vaguely resembling a human being, or the mockery of one.

Dr Frankenstein had nothing on them, Zahid's boss had joked once, and they had all forced a chuckle. Humour was armour. And there was no one there to hear them laugh at the awful, tasteless joke except for the dead.

Zahid didn't know how doctors could bear it: the screams and moans of the dying, the sobs and pleas of the living. At least the dead were quiet. The dead were well-behaved.

So when he heard a sound as he crept through the silent market, he froze for a moment. There weren't meant to be any sounds. That was one of the rules. The rescue teams went in first and retrieved the survivors so they could be taken to hospital, and then Zahid and his crew did the clean-up.

But there it was again: a sharp, frail cry, clear as morning.

A ghost, Zahid thought at once, still rooted in his place. It would be a ghost; this city was full of them. The afterlife was too crowded for so many dead, so their ghosts were left suspended over the buildings like low-hanging clouds, wispy bits of what had once been people, forever keeping watch over the living in their own personal version of hell.

It had to be a ghost, but the ghost cried out again, and it sounded like something that desperately wanted to live.

Gritting his teeth, Zahid followed the sound.

*

Come buy, come buy.
Come die, come die.
The world around them had cracked open like an egg on concrete, and now nothing outside existed. There was no more social media, no television, nothing but whispers and rumour carrying news from city to city. *We are no more,* they said, chimes of morose prophecy. *We are forgotten.*

But Zahid refused to forget the dead. He stepped over an arm protruding from the fragmented chunks of what had once been a structure he couldn't identify, now a disintegrating sculpture of wood and stone. It pained him to ignore it, that pitiful arm, but if the voice calling out truly wasn't a ghost, then he had to. The living took priority over the dead.

It sickened him that he had to remind himself of that. Perhaps this job had twisted something deep within him. Perhaps spending so much time around corpses had left him half-undead himself, a zombie of a man dragging his decaying parts behind him and groaning over the weight of them.

Again that sharp, frail cry. A baby bird fallen from its nest, a kitten crying for its mother. All the innocents of the world, crying out

39

with one voice. A child, Zahid's frantic mind reasoned. His heart shot out of his chest and danced ahead, urging him to go faster.

There.

There.

A tiny body. A little girl - he could see the red ribbons in her hair. A little girl who loved to play with dolls the way his sister had. In that fraction of a second, Zahid could see her entire past painted behind her, and the future that still twinkled, starlight-bright. Her parents would weep with joy when she was returned to them, even if she was covered in scars and would have nightmares for the rest of her life about the world exploding.

Better to live with nightmares, than to die and dream sweet dreams.

"I'm coming," Zahid called, his voice swallowed up by the market that had once been, but no longer was. "Here I am -"

His voice failed.

Those weren't red ribbons in her hair.

And she was no longer crying out. Perhaps she never had been. Perhaps she'd always been a ghost, leading him to her body, so her parents could put her to sleep for one final time.

Or so he told himself. The alternative, that he had been too late, that his momentary hesitation had cost him her life, was too horrible to contemplate.

*

"I think you should stop volunteering," his mother said, her fingers deft and gentle as they rubbed coconut oil into his hair.

Zahid said nothing, just tipped his head back against her knees and closed his eyes. The power was out. Candlelight washed the walls of their house in buttery yellow. The call to prayer warbled through a megaphone, crackly as a dying radio.

"It's not good for you, to be surrounded by the dead all the time. It does things to the mind."

Still Zahid stayed silent. He hadn't spoken since he'd returned home. He was afraid that if he opened his mouth, awful things would come spilling out, like that fairy tale about the girl who vomited out toads and snakes whenever she spoke.

"Your father's been talking to people," his mother added tentatively. "He says - there might be a way for us to leave. Flee across the border. There's a man who takes people in his truck, arranges all the paperwork. It's expensive, but -"

Living was expensive. Death was cheap. Zahid opened his eyes and smiled at her, and she seemed to soften at the sight of it, her fingers no longer digging into his scalp as if she was trying to keep his skull from cracking. He had seen a mother do that once, try desperately to hold the pieces of her child together, as if he was a jigsaw puzzle she needed to complete in order to get her son back.

It never worked. The pieces were scattered, lost to the wind.

"That would be nice," he said, the first and last lie he would ever tell his mother.

He could never leave. He would send his family in the trucks, but he would remain behind in this city that was no longer a city but a graveyard, picking through the pieces of the dead and putting them back together. So long as there were corpses, so would he remain, and finally they would have to bury what remained of him in the hungry, blood-soaked earth.

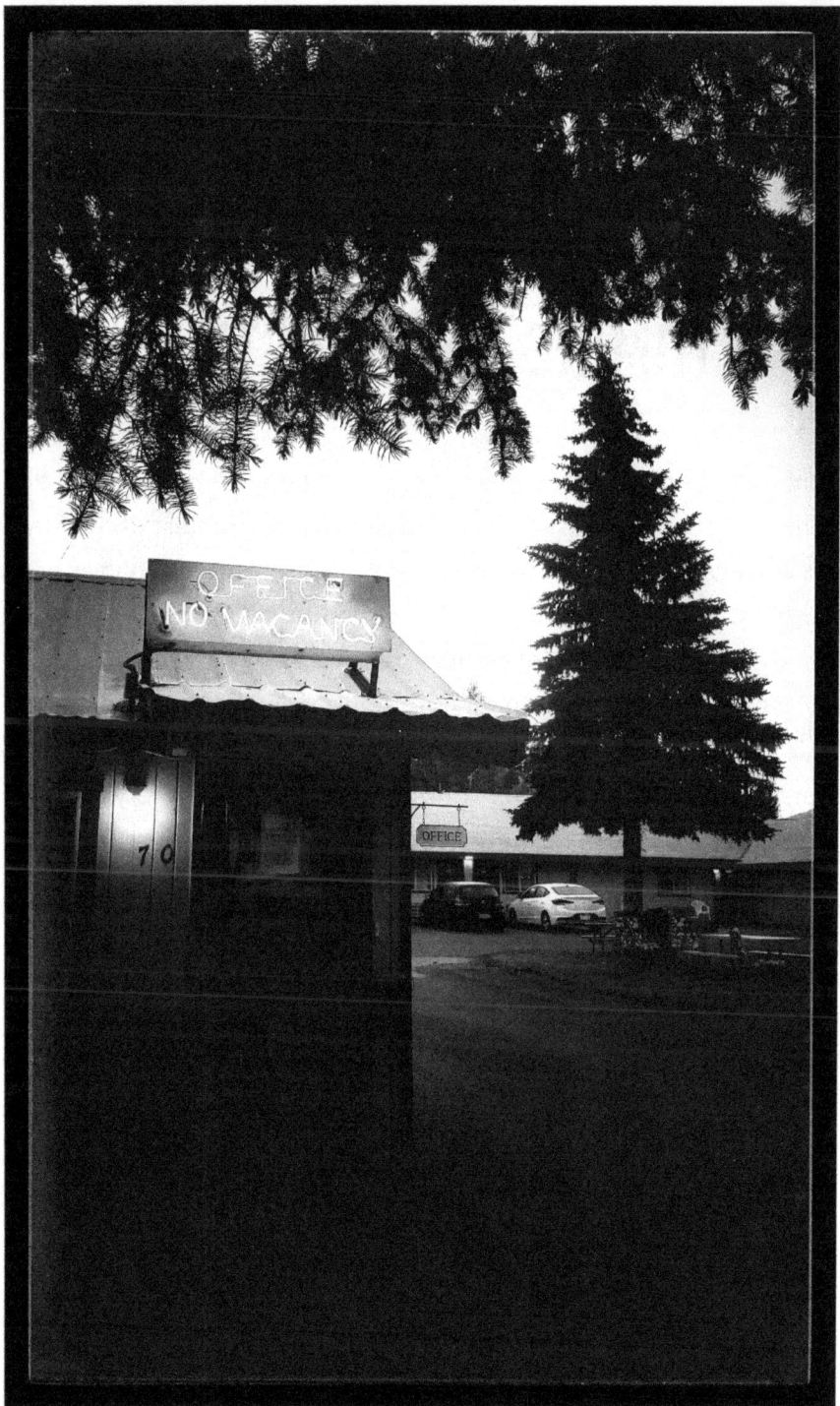

Kevin Grauke

LISTENING TO DYLAN THOMAS WHILE DRIVING THROUGH WYOMING ON CHRISTMAS EVE

With our children asleep in the backseat of our rental, we were driving through fog along the southern border of the emptiest of the fifty states on what can feel like either the most magical night of the year or the loneliest. We were heading from my sister's place in Utah to my wife's sister's place southeast of Denver. No one else was on the road but long-haul truckers far from their homes, families, and stockinged chimneys. The fog swirled in my headlights like the moaning phantoms outside Ebenezer Scrooge's window. As we've done every twenty-fourth of December, we were listening to Dylan Thomas's "A Child's Christmas in Wales," which he recorded in 1952, less than a year before he would famously die after downing eighteen straight whiskeys at the White Horse Tavern in Greenwich Village. His deep and comforting voice enveloped us, calling forth a cozy sea town flush with muffled and mittened postmen, uncles dozing in front of the fire, and snow, snow, so much snow. Besides the thrum of our tires on the asphalt and the low hush of heat sighing from the console vents, there was nothing else to hear. In a soundless whisper so as not to disturb my wife's absorption, I spoke my favorite lines along with him while remembering my own childhood Christmas Eves in snowless Texas listening to his warm voice with my parents, who instilled in me an early love for him. When, as an adult, I was able to drink at the bar of the White Horse Tavern, I closed my eyes and tried to feel him standing next to me.

Sometime after midnight, heavy-lidded on the outskirts of Laramie, I stopped for a coffee. Inside the gas station, an oasis of light in the blackness, Bing Crosby was singing "Silver Bells." A teenage boy stood behind the counter, the lone person there. When I pulled out my card to pay, he shook his head. "It's free tonight. Merry Christmas."

This took a second to register. "Really? Are you sure?"

He nodded. I wished him a Merry Christmas, as well, and returned to the rental, surprised at how affecting I found this small kindness in the middle of nowhere.

We still had hours to go before sleep. At least I did. My wife had joined my children in unconsciousness. Christmas morning in our matching pajamas at my sister-in-law's home would have to start a bit late. I drove on in silence through the foggy dark with the truck drivers, savoring the warmth of my thoughtful Christmas gift and thinking about the boy who'd given it to me, no doubt without his boss's permission. I hoped he had gifts waiting for him beneath a tree in a warm home close by.

Once the lights were finally out in our rented room in Parker and we were all tucked in tight, I heard again Dylan Thomas's last words as they faded into the digitized tape hiss of the original recording. I, too, said "some words to the close and holy darkness," and then I, too, slept.

Oladosu Michael Emerald

PERMISSION TO TALK ABOUT JOY & OTHER SOFT THINGS

They keep airing the footage: *another boy vanishing*
into the ocean like a name no one bothered to remember.
The headlines bruise the morning again: *a blast in the north,*
another mother folding into herself, grief gnawing
her name down to silence. The radio hums its tired dirge,
calls it breaking news—but it's the same flower
buried before bloom, the same garden of bones.
& maybe I've had enough of poems
that ache without relief, verses dressed in funerals.
I'm tired of the world's hunger for sorrow.
Today, I want to talk about beautiful things.
Happy things. Like this mango, golden meat slurped
straight from the bone. Like the old man dancing
to Apala in the rain, socks soaked, laughing
like the sky just told him a joke.
Like how the barbershop bursts with Black joy
on Saturdays when the Clippers win.
Like the small boy who cupped a dying bird
& sang to it until it stopped shivering.
Let me love the soft things. The dog's paw
resting on my open book. The boy who said,
I want to be a cloud because clouds

'don't get in trouble.' There's a field of sunflowers
that don't care who the president is.
The horse still runs like freedom never left.
I know the ache. I know how silence becomes
a second mouth. But I also know my mother's smile
when the bread rose in the oven—
that, too, is history. That, too, is worthy of record.
Tell me how delight is not resistance.
Tell me why I can't write about a woman
planting basil on the graves of her enemies
because she believes even bad men
deserve to be beautiful. For the bees.
I'm collecting joy like bottle caps,
each one a medal for surviving
without letting the world harden me.
Today I want to talk about the garden,
the one blooming behind the house you burned for warmth.
How even ash can nourish lilies.
How my uncle told me: *Joy is the bruise*
we press so it doesn't spread.
I stitched laughter into the hem of my sorrow.
My name is still a prayer. My hands still smell
like basil & sweat. Today, I'm giving myself
permission to smile. To laugh so hard
my sadness files a noise complaint.
To remember how Nana called Zoom *Zuma*
& we didn't correct her—the first time we saw her happy
since her dad left. We know the world is on fire,
but my nephew just spelled *hippopotamus*
on his first try, & that has to mean something.

So here's a poem that dances. That pours Fanta
over the tombstone. That wears yellow
even on a funeral day. You're allowed to feel good,
to sing off-key, to make pancakes shaped like failed
countries & eat them anyway.

PHOTOGRAPH BY JEFF BOGLE

PHOTOGRAPH BY JEFF BOGLE

Casey Jo Graham Welmers

ON LAKE MICHIGAN ALCHEMY (WITCHES' STONES)

Lake Michigan is electric in Caribbean blue, the waves charged and firing, giant monochromatic clouds shape-shifting over Christmas Cove Beach. I peel off my rash guard and slingshot it into the sand, shake the water from my hair and collapse into a tattered chair that pokes my bottom if I don't shift to the right. The beach is empty save for a pair of women nearby, rock hunters performing ritual bend and scoop prostrations. *Stoop, pause, scoop, AMEN.* Heavy canvas belt bags and metal strainers on long handles mark them as more than casual rock hounds. They sift through their cache, likely prioritizing finds: Petoskeys, Leland blues, beach glass. It's been at least two years since I was last here with my sister, Jodi, engaged in the same pursuit. No strainers, no bags, carefully focused on finding one stone and one stone only, all the rest collateral treasure. For us, it was always witches' stones.

*

Locally, they're called hag stones. Small quirky rocks with naturally eroded holes. Hole-y stones imbued with holy properties, nature's equivalent of an evil eye amulet, purported to offer healing, protection and a smattering of other ambiguous mystical qualities. But everything about 'hag' is ugly - the image invoked, the word on your tongue, the creep of it up your spine. Jodi and I defaulted to the slightly less pejorative 'witches' stone.' The first one we ever found was a smooth chunk of basalt punctuated with a comma of a hole. It was on Father's Day, ten years ago, our entire family trekking down a local beach, embracing summer and outdoor pursuits. Good Father's Day gifts are hard to come by, most stores littered with gaudy neck ties and cheap golf tchotchkes. But this gift was perfection, offered up so generously by the Lake herself. "It's the 'Grahamulet!'" I shouted, combining all the worst-best parts of dad humor to conjure this take on the family surname. My dad is a self proclaimed 'flaming atheist,' a man as far removed from religion as one can possibly be. That stone is the closest he will ever come to God. He tied it to a polished leather cord to wear around his neck, removing it rarely, if ever. Years later, he found himself abruptly airborne in the Arizona desert, ejected from his motorcycle by an older driver hauling, off all oddities in the desert, a boat trailer. His injuries were numerous: multiple broken ribs, facial fractures, a subdural hematoma. We were notified late at night via the flat tones of a hospital social worker with a poor connection. "He was transported via helicopter to Banner Health in Scottsdale," was the extent of information provided. We arrived at the hospital two flights and zero hours of sleep later. Dad had been upgraded to miraculously-doesn't-even-need-surgery status. Tucked into a corner of the ICU, I listened to beeping machines and turned his motorcycle helmet over in my hands. It was a sinister iteration of its previous form, the back side a cracked black egg. A plastic bag contained his clothes, black leather riding gear that had been cut into shreds of lifeless fabric. Dad cracked jokes with the occupational therapist, acing a test that required him to memorize a quantity of oranges. My held breath released then. I tracked the violet bruises and scarlet abrasions on his cheek, the IV lines criss-crossing into his arm. I carefully clocked the Grahmulet, settled like a protective bird on the chest of his faded checkered hospital gown.

*

Most of my memories from the fall of 2019 involve a music festival in Asbury Park, sea colored wind kites made to look like jelly fish pantomiming against sunset skies and black stages with giant speakers, all backdrop to an odd presage that there was a finalizing of something in my life. In my own morbid mind, I became convinced my husband and I would be victims of some tragic event, a shooting or an accident that would erase us from the Earth. My premonition was right, but it didn't pertain to me at all - it pertained to Jodi, who was diagnosed with stage 4 colorectal cancer at age 38. I remember a string of perpetual waiting. Waiting in sterile fluorescent exam rooms with thin paper sheets and surgical lounges with outdated blue vinyl chairs, waiting for the names of doctors to scroll across the screen of my tightly clutched phone, waiting for someone to slap my face, wake me up, end this shared nightmare. Because Jodi was young and healthy, her body responded well to surgery and six months of chemotherapy. But her mind was a Gordian knot, a psychic metastasis. Her visits to our favorite Lake Michigan beaches became small pilgrimages. Witches' stones were collected by the dozens and strung along a translucent thread of fishing line that hung from the curtain rod in her living room, a jagged strand of giant prayer beads. She notified me via text when her searches failed to produce results, always including a sad face for emphasis, a heartbreaking digital sort of resignation.

*

Jodi and I giggled at the red pin on my phone map marking a destination we had labeled 'Secert Beach,' because this is the goofy type of humor we delighted in; silly and stupid and funny to us alone. In one week she would have a second major surgery, an invasive procedure with an opaque outcome. We were headed to 'Secert Beach' to hunt for witches' stones. It was a secluded location, accessible only by dirt road and a set of wood-rotting stairs, the incomplete steps tumbling softly into the sand. Lake Michigan in early June was still crisp with the edge of summer. I shielded my eyes from the sun as Jodi walked behind me,

51

suddenly wishing I could turn over my palm and scoop it from the sky, wrap it around the two of us and let the rays scorch every last malignant molecule from her system. I imagine that's what any big sister and self-proclaimed protectress would desire. We passed a pile of stones that spelled out the word 'mom' and stopped in front of them to cry. Our own mother had been dead 20 years by then, so we took the meaning from them we needed, drawing a heart in the sand around the pebbled palindrome before continuing our search slowly, in tandem, seeking renewal from the lake and in the heft of small, peculiar stones.

*

Our childhood summers were a Midwest golden hour - a sepia toned, Great Lakes fueled, candy-sticky Polaroid. We built intricate sand castles and vaulted into Lake Michigan's thunderous waves, screeching in delight as our tiny bodies pummeled into the sand. We ate salty off-brand potato chips from hot foil bags and triangles of sticky pink watermelon from battered Tupperware bins, our hands and faces tacky messes the Lake would rinse clean, absolution for sweet and salty passions. Car rides home, windows down, were always enhanced by the hum of so many crickets, our backsides stamped with floral imprints of old bath towels repurposed for sitting in the car wearing still-wet swimsuits. We collapsed into our beds toasted brown from the sun, hair tangled, our sheets a cotton twist of sand and coconut scents. The rhythm of water is carried in human bones, a fact I assign to the deep sleep of a childhood spent in the waves. Coiled like a sun-kissed nautilus atop our shared bunk, I imagined my heart as a melting thing, seeping through the mattress and pooling below, into the lower bed where Jodi slept. It was the energy of the Lake in my blood, a life force and a love force, a current always moving through me. Lake Michigan has a sacred alchemy. An ability to destruct and create, an alchemy perfectly embodied in witches' stones. As a child I would have been incapable of articulating this knowing, but it was inherent - settled in my bones alongside the memory of water.

*

I divined a perfect witches' stone that day on 'Secert Beach' with Jodi. I will never know if this was sheer luck or cosmic alignment, the stars we wished on taking pity on our small, desperate forms. The stone was solid and thick, at least the size of a walnut with a hole larger than a paper punch through a gray and ochre core. I christened it the 'Sister Stone,' the eons of time and energy for this small miracle to find us racing like a whipping film sprocket through my mind. Our initial excitement over this discovery devolved quickly into sticky, tearful clutching. "Because I found this, it's from me, it's a part of me, and when you wear it you'll know I'm with you! Even when I'm not there," I babbled, thrusting the stone at her thin chest, willing the best of my being into its invisible pores.

*

Jodi wore the stone through her major surgery, through months of clinical trials and a last-ditch procedure to attack the aggressive tumors that had by then infiltrated her liver. She was wearing the stone when she left this life 16 months later on a warm morning in November, the last warm day of the year. I had cranked all the windows open for the balmy weather, but also because old folklore demands this when someone passes away. Jodi hated winter. It made complete sense that she would make her exit before the snow fell, a small gasping. I washed her shattered body with sandalwood, clary sage and water from a spring near the Lake. Her best friend had collected it at my request, in gallon size plastic milk jugs, the sacred temporarily housed in the mundane. I clutched the Sister Stone in a sweaty vice grip over her still heart. Lines from the Grateful Dead's "Ripple" played in her room as family sat with her, holding vigil, holding on, grasping, gripping, slipping. It was a recording Jodi and I had made together, me playing ukulele and the two of us singing, heads shuttling back and forth in synchrony. Dad cradled Jodi's head in his hands, kept repeating that she looked so beautiful now, like a princess. And she really did - like a princess from a mystical desert planet or another place and time, her head hooded in muslin, hair cascading out, silver discs with intricate designs dangling from her ears. For the past two weeks her mouth had been gnarled in a downward twist of pain, but now, released, she wore a small, quiet smile. I grabbed that smile like a life raft, clutched to it as I stared at her bedroom walls, a blue grey color, a color like water rushing and carrying us all away.

*

It's a particular shade of lavender, the color of the sky at dusk that strikes me most. Something between purple and blue yet not indigo or periwinkle. It's faintly pink around the edges, a tinge. The color of the place I go to in my mind when I think of Lake Michigan after sunset in early September, the moon a white slice. It's Jodi and I beneath that sky on an old tie-dye sheet, attempting to eat enchiladas verdes in the lingering twilight, our blue jeans rolled up, the cuffs tiny baskets of white sand that will later trickle out into our cars and bedrooms and other corners of our life. It's sand I'll find months later and gather with a finger or toe into a tiny pile, and the color of the spell I wish I possessed to be able to see her once again. Jodi did not fail some epic cancer battle and the witches' stone did not fail in protecting her. All of it was magic that simply transmuted in ways only the magician can know. The following July I paddled her board out into the Lake, scarlet begonias trailing off the side, family and friends gathered at the shore and in the water, up to their knees, up to their chests. It was a sublime day at our favorite semi-secret beach, the place I connect with that particular shade of lavender. We had it entirely to ourselves. I leaned over the side, shaking and hesitant, finally releasing her stone into the aquamarine expanse. The last line of the song "Ripple" is a wishing to know how to take someone home. I have listened to it hundreds of times by now.

*

The two rock hunters nearby are now combing carefully through a newly collected strainer full of stones. Their heads bend toward each other in a similar and familiar fashion, the space between them not a space at all. *Sisters*, I think. The motion that happens next is instinctual, my hand rushing toward my heart, my fingers dancing around the crooked oval that hangs there, a witches' stone. Their formation varies based upon material and geographical locale, but my favorite origin story is this: a smaller stone comes into contact with a larger stone. After years of assistance from wind, water and sand, the smaller stone eventually erodes through the larger stone and viola - a witches' stone is formed. I was once blessed to have another human in my life who embedded herself next to me. Who for 39 years was an integral part of my existence until one day she passed through me, departing for waters unknown, leaving a cavernous hole where she once so snuggly fit. I have been brilliantly, achingly, destroyed. I have been alchemized into something new.

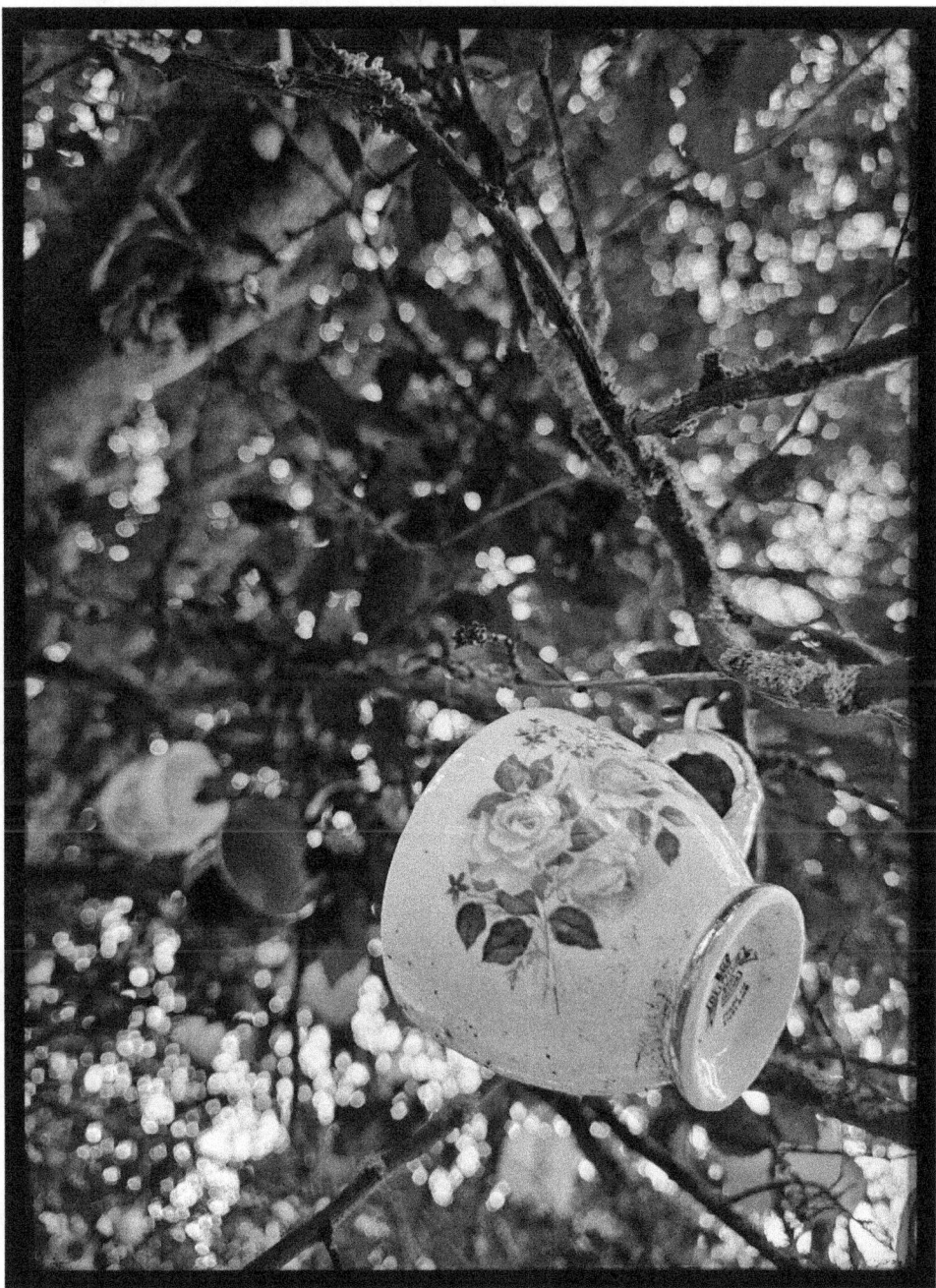

PHOTOGRAPH BY JEFF BOGLE

Susan Kolon

PEP TALK

I hate going in here, I ruin
my manicure, bite my thumbs
down to dead tissue.

Aunt Dorothy said, *get out
to where the men get out*
and that's The Cow Pony.

Much better than my date last night
with the couch, crushing
bamboo bowls of stove popcorn,

reading twelve greasy pages over
and over without comprehension,
my mood turning to charcoal.

Don't expect a prince, look
for a brute you can take the edge
off. You did it with your feral cat...

The bathroom line is a spectator sport;
you watch bros on barstools.
At the other end of that fist pump

might be a shoulder broad enough
to carry your burdens. The guy
with armpit sweat might propose

moving Dad's gun safe two flights
down to the basement's concrete
floor. Will I always be haunted

by that rando, *You have a banging
body, butterface? Wait, it was
a compliment!* Remember

when you blew up Becky's
Bunsen burner at Camp O-Ongo?
Boys thought you were cool

because you walked around
flicking your Dad's Zippo –
do that tonight.

You don't need attention to feel
ha, yes you do; lower the key
of *Girls Just Wanna Have Fun*.

You're too nice to shut anyone
down, too plain-looking to say
no to a pity drink.

Maybe tonight is the night
someone might say,
My parents are going to love you.

THE HOT PANTS RULE

It's a damn shame, the state of public school funding – all the bake sales and pledge drives, the parents selling raffle tickets for a refurbished iPad. Nobody wants the refurbished model; everyone wants the latest. Kennedy Elementary, at least, has the right idea, a glimmer of the spirit of innovation. Sure, the entrance fee is steep ($50 a pop), but the experience of going to a roller disco in one's old grade school? Priceless. The ground rules are simple: no hot pants with an inseam of less than two inches, no drugs or booze (detectable, anyway): basically, the same rules as regular school. The hot pants rule is the only one regarding dress, and I wear my shimmer leggings and the ancient Bevis & Butthead tee that my mom used to clean bathrooms before I rescued it from the rag heap.

After the final bell, the custodians swap out all those fluorescent tubes with strobes and blacklights. Principal Dooley pulls up her hidden Spotify playlists, draws her work-issued laptop as near to the PA as it'll go, sways in time as Donna Summer's voice warbles through the dusty hallways.

I'm years removed from this space – let's be real: decades – but as I glide through the corridors, I can't ignore the little ghost scenes my psyche carries. The water fountain where Mr. Grunewald, cutup art teacher, dunked his trout tie in the water pooling the gum-clogged basin. The music room risers behind which Phil K yanked his Umbros down to show everybody his ween. The library – that low-ceilinged, beige refuge – whose periodicals were all at least six months out of date.

The other rule, the one I almost always forget, is to leave all objects & artifacts in their original states. Drifting along the art hall with all the speed a middle-aged woman can muster, I long to run my hands over the fingerpaint portraits tacked there by the kindergarteners, the dimpled paper and globby pigment the ultimate texture of trying, failing. I don't, though. I skate on, with each thrust of my legs whispering, "no touching, no touching."

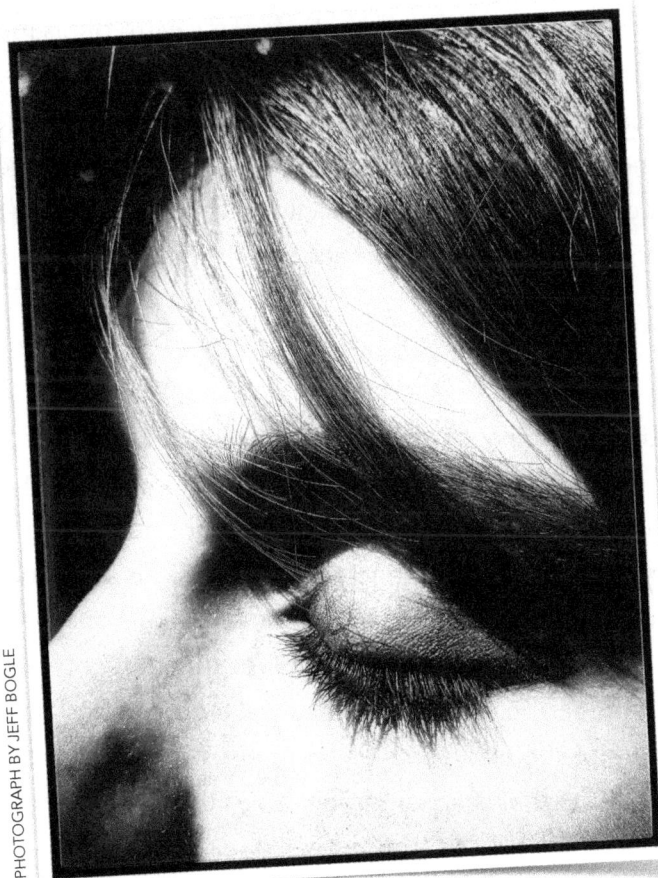

PHOTOGRAPH BY JEFF BOGLE

EXTRACTION

Sean was the smartest kid in my class at Granite Valley Correctional Facility. I say kid, but I don't know exactly his age. He looked weathered. His skin was lined and dry, it had a thickness to it that most likely came from exposure to the elements, extreme cold, wind. He didn't have his four front upper teeth. His smile disarmed me; he was quite handsome so seeing only his gums, and into the cavern of his mouth, was hard to reconcile with his good looks. Sean had thick black hair. His eyes were equally dark; they were shining and there was an eagerness to them, a hunger. That's why I thought of him as a kid: he seemed excited for so much, as if the future was still full of real and dazzling possibility, but also frustrated by and impatient with what was standing in his way.

**

A small jittering shadow. A mirage. Limbs bending in impossible directions casting otherworldly images on white walls turned beige from time and dirt. It is night. But it is not quiet: It is never quiet here. The watchman's keys jangle. There are sighs and moans that bounce off the concrete walls and ceiling, the emissions of men in cages seeking the smallest bit of solace. Or the residue of nightmares that most can't remember but from which they wake groggy and unsettled. Some can't help but sob as dreams of being elsewhere collide with the reality of caged life that sharpens into view as they pull away from slumber.

**

Sean talked about his teeth in class. I had introduced the idea of social norms and deviance, something these students were experts on, but they weren't always able to identify it in their experiences. Sean got everything quickly. The guys in this makeshift jail classroom didn't raise their hands, they spoke when they wanted to. Sean started talking. I am sure my eyes widened and I blushed; I always thought of his teeth as a topic to avoid. They were another sign of poverty that stood in contrast to the healthy ski-tanned, farm-to-table idea of Vermont that is one of its main exports and to the well-fed good looks of the athletic students at the private liberal arts college an hour up the road where I worked. My jail students looked my age – late 40's – but all of them, I later found out, were a few decades younger than me, another effect of a life of neglect and abuse and opiates and cigarettes, childhoods spent in cold isolation, often raised by foster parents who handed them back to the state when they inevitably turned into troubled teens.

**

In this place where no one will ever be so defeated that they call it home, Sean is weeping for his dead dog, run over by the friend he entrusted her to. When he looks out the barred slit of a window, sees the sky turning pale, streaked with pink, as he hears the guards rumbling, he covers his eyes with his forearm, like a cat keeping the light out. His feet are crossed and shaking. He is lying on top of his itchy wool blanket; he is hot and sticky from feeling.

**

Sean told us that his court-assigned social worker had arranged for a dentist to give him implants. The dentist would have to extract some more teeth before giving him new ones, she explained. Sean didn't want them. The social worker, a young woman who I sometimes saw in the jail's glass-walled visiting room – she had long straight blonde hair, smooth skin– had recently graduated with a bachelor's degree from a nearby state college. She was angry at Sean when he refused the help she arranged. "I look good the way I am!" he told her. She wrote a report in his file indicating that she did not think he could be rehabilitated. All the guys I was teaching hadn't been convicted yet. They were waiting for their day in court with their public defenders who would encourage them to plead guilty in exchange for probation or a prison sentence. Sean had already spent almost a year fighting his charges. He told me several times that he was innocent. This report from the social worker could derail his efforts to get free.

After Sean finished the story of his teeth, there was silence. The guys looked down at their desks. The problem with sociology is that there is often understanding but no resolution and I didn't want to leave any of these guys worse off. "It's all about power," Sean said. I told him that there is a subfield of sociology dedicated to the topic of power. He asked me if I'd come back and teach a class about that. "I'd like to." I meant this. But I also wanted Sean to be out or somewhere else, no longer in limbo.

Covid would keep me away from the jail for several years and I never found out what happened to the guys from that January semester. One of them, a sweet and very polite fresh-faced kid from Brooklyn, who state police caught driving drugs up to Canada for a girl he liked, got moved to a federal facility; with an almost certain conviction and at least a decade sentence ahead of him, I assume he's still in prison. He wanted to go to college when he got out. Sean, too, wanted to go to college. And then law school. He had learned so much preparing his own defense in jail, he told me, that he one day wanted to help free guys like him.

**

The guards run their rubber batons on the metal bars of the cells. Sean does not stir. He feels the hot breath of the morning guy hissing at him to "Get the fuck up," but grief shackles Sean to his bed. He hears urgent excited voices that sound simultaneously close and far. In a few seconds he will be the first real case at this small jail, nestled between an elementary school and a cemetery, for guards newly trained in the state-of-the art technique of cell extraction.

**

I taught a four-week class. The guys came and went, often being released to community supervision or sent upstate or out of state to prison, so they were a rotating group. Some guys showed up mainly to get out of their cells, see the sky and breathe some fresh, if freezing, air on the walk to this outbuilding. Sean was the only consistent student. He always looked at me, concentrating, telling the other guys to be quiet or settle down if they got bored or rambunctious. I didn't give the students any reading. The jail's education coordinator, Carl, had warned me that articles or books would be destroyed in the cells by jealous roommates or resentful guards. So, I did a lot of talking, introducing ideas and explaining. Sean always stared with focus, asking questions for clarifications. For this reason, I was surprised when he missed the penultimate class. The conversation deflated without him. During the break, Carl told me that Sean's dog had died; too sad to move, he refused to leave his cell so the guards had to force him out. "You should see what they did to his face!" Carl chuckled. I said something like "that's horrible" or "oh, poor guy," and Carl replied, "If you saw what Sean did to his wife's face, you wouldn't feel an ounce of pity for him." I had told Carl many times that I didn't want to know what the guys were arrested for but he saw himself in the role of translator, making sure the liberal white lady from the rich college in the fancy town 35 miles north understood she was teaching monsters. I never knew what Carl thought of me, but on my last day, he took me to lunch - we ate meatball subs - and he said he would miss me. I like to think that I, and he, and the guys, had all transcended our stereotypes but it's hard in a place like this.

**

Three men grab at Sean's slight frame. Two hold him like a paper doll, his arms and legs move as if made of wire springs, while the third uses his baton on Sean's face and chest. Sean's silence infuriates, his limp body enrages. They roar at him. He stares wide eyed as if they are speaking a foreign tongue. They throw him back in his cell; he's too messy for breakfast now, it will unsettle the others.

**

On the final day of class, I brought in two boxes of donuts from a local bakery, making sure to offer some to the guards as I walked through the metal detector, past the main security desk, down the long hall to the door that a guard opened to take me outside and into the education building. The guys came in about ten minutes later. I saw Sean: his cheek was swollen, his eyes were purple and puffy. He looked exhausted. "Welcome back!" I said with forced cheer. "I wasn't feeling up for class yesterday," he said. He seemed subdued but excited for a donut. He took one out of the box. It was raspberry or blueberry jelly. His hands trembled. As he went to put the donut on the paper plate I had put next to the box, he dropped it on the floor. Its insides oozed onto the gray carpet. I told him that I had brought extra, he could take another. "It's okay, I don't have much of an appetite anyway, Professor."

**

Sean lies down on his bed, blood working its way into the coarse fibers of the blanket. He turns on his side, his trembling foot making a small jittering shadow on the wall.

**

The story of Sean's cell extraction has stuck in my mind for years. One day, during those four weeks, when there weren't enough guards to monitor the education building, my class had to meet in the visiting room. As we talked, several very large men, tall and wide, walked by, wearing bullet proof vests and carrying rubber batons and plexiglass face shields. They looked out of place at this small rural jail where the guards were average sized, some out of shape, many near retirement. The guys sat around a seminar style oval table. The ones who could see the men walk past stopped talking; the ones with their backs to the glass instinctively knew something was going on so they turned around to see. Carl later told me they were there to professionalize the guards, turn them into corrections officers.

I have tried to imagine what happened in those few minutes in the cell of one of my smartest and favorite students, as I navigated icy roads and snow in my VW Golf on my hour ride south to the jail. I've written this story many times, in different ways. People who have read it tell me they "want more of Sean." Or that they need to know about the friendship between Sean and the guy he gave his dog to; some backstory to make him sympathetic or believable. But, I don't have that story and I cannot seem to make it up. I don't imagine it's that unique or that it matters, really. Sean, and many of the guys I taught, had no chance in life, coming from poor families in a poor town in a state that treated them as a failed social experiment, bouncing them between foster care, drug treatment, jail and probation, just like their parents had been.

I like to think that Sean went to community college, but it's unlikely he did; that he got out of his own way, to make a better life for himself, but chances are he didn't. And maybe I wonder if he occasionally thinks of our month together, though I'm certain it pre-occupies me far more than it does him. I doubt he could imagine that the violence surrounding him still haunts his professor, with whom he talked eagerly about big ideas, wearing the gap-toothed grin I also like to think he still has.

Bob King

I'VE BEEN A PROFESSOR AT A PUBLIC UNIVERSITY FOR THE PAST 27 YEARS & THE STATE OF OHIO FINALLY ENACTED A LAW TO PREVENT ME FROM INDOCTRINATING STUDENTS

The first student I made cry
wept as I explained that the Bible isn't an academically reputable source
for this particular assignment
& anyhow Jesus Christ does not, in fact,
belong in the author's slot on the Works Cited for this text.
No, I'm not saying he couldn't hit a curveball.
No, I'm not saying you shouldn't follow him from
the on-deck circle. Thank god *only one* I can count
on fewer than a full hand of fingers
the number of students who have lost their lives
by their own hands.
Two of them because their
families couldn't support whom they loved,
& they were ultimately convinced that they
couldn't ever find love in this world, so they
got a jump start on the next,
& at the wake their family asked me *why*
& I said, I'm just a teacher a father a few atoms
of empathy hastily incarnated,
& not really qualified to answer that question,
at least here & now, & goddamnit Sarah,
I wish I could've helped you more.

VIEWFINDER

When I was fourteen and knew everything, my father showed up at school unannounced one day. His intention was to pry my head from my ass so I wouldn't repeat the eighth grade, and he thought the best way of doing that was deer hunting near Mexico.

In the school parking lot, his truck was packed with everything we needed for the weekend—tent, sleeping bags, rifles, the camo jacket my brother outgrew. My brother had gone hunting with my father regularly since well before junior high, but he always did have the disposition of an Eagle Scout. On the other hand, I did not. Back then, my personality revolved around suspensions for fights I usually started, or getting grounded so I could catch up on the homework I never did. As my mother put it, as a kid I was always more concerned with keeping my eyes on everything but the fact that I was blowing the kind of opportunity my father worked a steady stream of overtime to provide.

At the turnoff for Picacho Peak, Dad pulled over at the gas station and bought two chocolate Drumsticks and a map of southern Arizona. In the car, he tossed me the map, and while I licked the ice cream before it melted, he told me to figure out where we were going.

"But you already know where you're going," I said. "It's the same place you take Chris."

My father checked his mirrors and merged between Peterbilts heading south on the 10.

"Just unfold the map."

Getting us to Tucson was easy—it was a straight shot down the interstate from Phoenix—and somehow I got us to Tombstone, then Bisbee, and finally Douglas after that. At the Walmart, we filled our cooler with groceries, Dad handing me the list on our way in and telling me to grab what we needed while he picked up sandwiches at the Subway inside the store. Afterward, he drove me to see the border. I don't think he even put the truck in park before he used his police voice—which he normally kept at work but started using more and more around the house with every report card I brought home--when I jumped out and made a beeline for the fence that randomly ended past the last house of the neighborhood. Beyond it, open desert without end.

"But I want you to take my picture on the other side," I said after he demanded I stop.

"Well, you can go around that fence if you want," he said, then pointed to the green Tahoe parked down the road. "But I don't think they'll let you come back if you do."

From Douglas we drove dirt roads for an hour until Dad made me hop out and open a barbed wire cattle gate. It was another thirty minutes before he pulled through a thicket of mesquite.

"These'll give us good shade," he said, and cut the engine after parking beside the trees. He made me unpack our stuff while he reclined in an old aluminum lawn chair. When I reached for the rifle cases, he told me to leave those where they were. He pointed at the shovel and wooden box with the hole cut on top, which he normally kept in a black garbage bag in our shed. "Go set that up over there," he said, and thumbed over his shoulder. "These trees'll give us good privacy, too."

The next morning we left camp after breakfast, broken fried eggs Dad had me make in a skillet over the campfire. We took the truck up a desert mountain road, Dad pulling over every few minutes to look through his binoculars.

"There," he said, pointing.

I nodded and said "yeah," like I knew what he was pointing at.

We parked the truck in a ditch and slid through the crispy brush into a dry creek bed that ran alongside the road, and which I hadn't realized was even there until we were in it.

"Look," Dad said, pointing. But I still didn't see what he was talking about. Only after we got home and he told my mother about the trip did I understand he'd been showing me tracks in the soil. Scat. Broken mesquite branches and rubbed fur on the trees.

We didn't see a deer all day. We saw empty gallon jugs and used toilet paper and discarded sneakers, their soles torn asunder from the toe. But no deer. No javelina. Nothing.

"Look," Dad kept saying, but I didn't see shit.

I don't know how long we meandered through that dry creek bed, but it felt like forever hunched under the trees, thorny brush snagging our camo pants and scraping our ankles bloody. When we emerged, we were on the other side of the mountain. Dad sat on a rock overlooking the valley. He took off his hat and wiped the sweat from his forehead, then rested his M1 Garand—which my grandfather had used in Europe a lifetime before—across his lap, his mouth drooping in search of breath. I drank from my canteen and wiped my mouth with the back of my hand. In the valley, a group of tiny people filed into a van that was no bigger than a Hot Wheel at such distance.

I couldn't tell what those people were doing in the middle of the desert, so I raised my rifle—the Winchester .30-30 Dad got from my mother as a wedding gift—to peer through the scope for a better look. The second I did though, white sky filled my view as my father yanked the Winchester upward from my hands.

"Don't do that," he said, holding the rifle. "Not like that. I'll lend you my binoculars if you want." Through his binoculars, we watched the last person file into the van. I couldn't believe how many fit. Then a thick cloud of dust kicked up behind the vehicle as it lurched up and down across the cracked desert floor. I didn't understand why anyone would willfully put themselves through something like that. When the van disappeared and only a haze of dirt hung in the air, Dad stood and said, "You hungry?" and we headed back to the truck without a word.

The next morning we walked a grazing field where some hunters we'd met on the road said they'd seen a herd move through the night before. They told us they'd be out there themselves if they hadn't already filled their tag.

Brass shells shone dully on the ground as we crossed the field and the sun crossed above us. This is .30-06, Dad told me, picking up a shell to show me. This is .308. This is 7.62 x 39mm. "Whoever shot that was probably just using an SKS," Dad said as he flicked the brass into the desert. I nodded like I knew what he was talking about. Near lunch, I found an owl skull which I still have today. But no deer. Not even tracks for deer. We never caught a single wind of what we had come all that way to find.

At camp, we shot our rifles at empty cans of soup and other things previous hunters had abandoned. Crushed Budweisers. A cooking pan. Afterward, by Coleman lantern light, Dad taught me how to clean our rifles. How to disassemble and oil their parts so they'd work properly next time. I had school in the morning, so we broke camp after dinner—steaks my father had packed in ice and made me grill over the campfire on a cast iron grate he'd brought with us.

"Don't flip them yet," he told me. "Let them simmer. You'll know when they're good."

Somehow, the dirt road back to Douglas felt less bumpy than it had on the way in. After I opened the cattle gate, the moon bright above us, I hopped in the truck and fidgeted with the radio, Mariachi music fading in and out to symphony music on the same channel. I was still messing with the dials when Dad nudged me. In the peripherals of our headlights, a deer stood on the side of the road as we passed it.

"Wait," I yelled. I twisted in my sweat to get a better look, only for the animal to disappear into the darkness beyond our taillights. I unbuckled my belt and told Dad to turn around, go back, when my stomach lurched and the truck eased us toward a gentle stop. Outside, more deer stood on the side of the road. Dozens of them. Dozens.

We sat there idling until Dad shifted the truck in park. In quiet contemplation, he pressed his calloused thumb to his chapped lip. He turned his head slowly back and forth in thought. I had seen that look a lot lately, whenever he was at his wit's end figuring out what to do after Mom got another call from my teacher, or when my basketball coach kicked me off the team for mouthing off, or when some parent called during dinner to relay every bad thing their child reported I had said or done during the day, me simply refusing to see what I was becoming.

At the edge of our headlights, a doe gingerly crossed the road. "Let's get the rifles," I said.

"Our tags don't extend past the gate."

We kept sitting there, until I motioned to put my seatbelt back on. Instead, I let go of the strap. I opened my door, the gravel crunching under my boots. Under the dome light, Dad shifted in his seat toward me. All the deer watched from the shadows. The air was cold. The doe lifted her head, her eyes bright in the reflection of our headlights.

"Look at them, Dad," I said. "Jesus, look at them all."

PHOTOGRAPH BY JEFF BOGLE

Tracie Adams

THE TIME LOOP IS NOT A METAPHOR

My childhood is a time loop, and this is not a metaphor. It is as real as the sun-warmed breakfast cereal I eat at my grandmother's kitchen table where every morning my tiny legs dangle and tangle, too tiny to touch the linoleum tiles. It is as real as the long days of summer, every day and every year the same. I am six years old, picking turnips from Grandpa's garden, looping my bike's banana seat and tasseled handlebars through quiet neighborhood streets until the church bell rings five times and I know Mama has dinner ready.

My childhood is a time loop, and this is not a metaphor. I imagine you are skeptical that the time loop is real because it is so good at metaphoring. I assure you, it is very real. I would start at the beginning, but who can say for sure where a beginning ends or an ending begins?

My childhood is a time loop, and this is not a metaphor. I eat breakfast, I go to Grandma's, every night I'm a burrito wrapped in pink floral blankets. Every night, Mama is tired from standing on her feet doing perms at the hair salon, but she serves us dinner, even if it is just a sandwich on rye bread. Every night, she turns out my light and kisses me goodnight. Every day, every summer, every year. This is how real the time loop is. Until it isn't.

Suddenly, my childhood is NOT a time loop, and this is not a metaphor. Every day is different. Sometimes I ride my bike and listen for the bells. Sometimes I pack a suitcase to spend the weekend with my father. Sometimes I lie in that sterile room with no toys, waiting for footsteps, waiting for my father to come to my bed, to kiss me on my mouth and on my legs, so tiny, too tiny to understand why this is what my father must do to me so that he can be happy. It makes my stomach ache, and this is very real.

My childhood is NOT a time loop, and this is not a metaphor. The days are all different now, and some of them make my stomach ache, so I twist my hair and that helps a little. And because my childhood is NOT a time loop, tomorrow will not be the same as today. But I remember it all, every beginning and every ending.

D.E. Hardy

LEAVE ONLY FOOTPRINTS

We watch Tourist Dad short the turn into the parking lot, his Cruise America's front wheel hopping the curb, making the dog decal plastered on the side jump. Such a good boi, forever panting like he's on the ride of his life. Tourist Dad parks in the middle of the main lane, hops out of the cab, and bounds into the rental office. He's jaunty and talky and full of vacation memes, saying he only loves his job when he's on vacation. He asks, Am I right? We say, So right. He asks for the open spot closest to the ocean. Classic Tourist Dad request. We give him the space without cluing him to the fact that the California coastline near the Oregon border is cold as fuck. He parks between another Cruise America and a freshly buffed Airstream.

Tourist Dad and Tourist Son, probably the oldest of the Tourist kids, get out and take a lap around the park. They walk from the ocean to the Marina that's not the flashy-yachty kind, more the boat-can-technically-float kind, then from the Marina to the street to the row of shops that abut the office. We watch Tourist Dad double-take the sushi restaurant next to the aquarium store. He mouths *ironic* to Tourist Son and chuckles at his own joke. That's nothing, we think, wait till he gets a load of the monument maker's shop on the far side of the lot. Sample tombstones lined up, rows and rows of granite, sleek and orderly rectangles, kind of like an RV park. On the walk back to their Cruise America, we watch Tourist Dad encounter Tony, one of the monthlies, who's on speaker phone. Tony's been a little low lately, but nothing he can't handle, and now, he stands outside in his boxers, undershirt, and a dingy terry bathrobe. The caller announces chicken's on sale. Tony yells into his device that chicken tears him up inside. The caller says, yeah, but it's on sale. Tony says, okay, but I warned you. Tourist Dad looks up and down the row he's in. Some RVs don't have wheels anymore, others are rusting out at the windows, the one next to Tony sports a makeshift fence of oil drums turned into planters, which is clever if you think about it, resourceful, but Tourist Dads seem to find this home improvement a bridge beyond their comfort. This Tourist Dad quickens his step. His Tourist Son giggles. So do we. Tourist Son isn't going to be allowed outside his RV again.

Later, Tourist Dad comes back to the office. Wind's on now, and he's got his Patagonia zipped high to protect his ears. This isn't his regular fleece, we can tell. No pills, no worn patches, clean zipper. His regular Patagonia is black, we bet. Black Patagonia is the official fleece of Work Dad. But Tourist Dad isn't Work Dad today, so he's wearing his fun Patagonia. This one's teal. So fun. Tourist Dad asks about quarters for the laundry and bottles of water and grocery stores. Then Tourist Dad wonders if we know of an artisanal butter shop. We don't. A buddy of his once found one somewhere around here that sells edible butter candles. Tourist Dad says, They really make roasted artichokes novel again, you know? We nod. So novel. We overcharge Tourist Dad for the water and write down "edible butter candle." The night crew is not going to believe this one. We can't wait to tell them.

Tourist Dad's registration sheet says there's also a Tourist Mom and two more Tourist Kids, but we never see them. Just Tourist Dad walking to the market, Tourist Dad back and forth from the laundry, Tourist Dad staring at the ocean, the wind blowing the Tourist Zen right out of him. When we clock back in the next day, Tourist Dad is the first one to the office. He knows he's paid for three nights, but can he get a refund? He cannot. We say, Sunk cost, my dude, sunk cost. We say, You can always make money, you can't always make memories, right? He says, So right. We watch his Cruise America pull away, dog decal happy as ever. We wave so long to Tourist Family. We recite our favorite meme: a vacation is having nothing to do and all day to do it in. We sit back and watch the waves beat the rocks at the edge of the lot.

PHOTOGRAPH BY JEFF BOGLE

Valeria Eden

ANTI-ODE TO GIRLHOOD

after Olivia Gatwood

to blood,
smeared lipstick, the ruptured
vessels of our bodies

that bloom on borrowed time,
our anger the only thing we own,
  and to the color red
      that never leaves us,

how we make aching an art form,
howl at the moon
      and hold rituals
in public bathrooms using girl-tears
in place of holy water,

giving birth to each other even
if we have never been mothers,
our girl-ness the only qualification
we need to be of each other,
      ripe and
bursting from the wound of it,

how we are *so* multifaceted in our talent,
always overachieving,
      somehow
both the life of the party and
also, always,   the headline,

     the deer,
the body in the alley tucked behind a dumpster,
blue-lipped and cold,

how even in death we look out for one another,
our lost sisters never silent,
     they are lessons
     and warnings,
their soundless screams like scripture,

the tender flesh of their ruined mouths
     left open
and fossilized into something
every
    girl
       can hear.

BELOW ZERO DAYS

. . . .

Trash day again. Every week. Means the weeks are slipping through my fingers like sand. Like water, something that moves past skin without much resistance. I have to haul the bins from the side of the house to the street. Over driveway, over snow. I should shovel the driveway, but I don't. The ice block that is our street.

She hasn't told me what my consequence is.

~

"You shouldn't go out there with wet hair," she says.

"I'll be fine," I say.

"It's below zero," she says. "Anything wet will freeze in minutes."

"Why do you care?" I ask

She shrugs.

Outside, my hair freezes. An ice helmet fitted to my skull. I return to the house and climb into the bathtub. Run the water hot as it can go.

~

Sunday, and I know she wants me in church. I don't go to church. Don't believe in god. And besides that, I've told her a dozen times, I'm Jewish. She always looks at me then, squints and turns away, like I'm too bright to look at. Or like she's trying to figure me out. Like she doesn't understand how a person can be Jewish and not believe in god. Or she doesn't believe that church isn't right for everyone.

Church isn't right for her. I've seen the way she looks at me, eyes hungry for something else.

~

The problem is she doesn't know herself. Not really. And she was raised here in Indiana to love god and country and all the things she knows I don't believe in. She's just a room to rent: I have to remind myself. I found her on Craigslist. $500 with utilities. In Broad Ripple.

I'm an anomaly to her. My tattoos, my Bernie Sanders poster. My California blonde hair and my California attitude.

She leaves me post it notes: *Please place pot lids in pot lid holder.* And she places utility bills on my pillow, circling the cost of gas and writing *this is the water heater.*

In other words, I'm a bit haphazard and I take too many baths.

~

The bigger problem: weeks ago at a bar. She's drunk off two fishbowl cocktails. Really drunk.

"Have you ever—you know—experimented?"

I laugh. "How?"

"You know." She looks around and lowers her voice. "With another—you know."

"A woman." I say.

She nods, her eyes wide as the world she's afraid of.

"Sure," I say, thinking of a woman I dated a few years back. Julia, like the Beatles song.

"And?" she asks.

"And what?" I say.

"And did you know—like do—?"

"Like did we fuck?"

She stiffens and pulls away from me. She's not one for swearing. God, etc. "Never mind," she says.

"Sorry," I say. "I'm happy to talk—"

"No need," she says.

And that was it. The end. And now, she won't look at me.

~

Another trash day. The post it notes are accumulating. *Please turn me off,* the one on the coffeemaker reads. Almost too on the nose. I'd laugh, but I feel a little sad instead. I deposit the note in the trash along with a handful of yellow squares. I drag the bins over the snow. I'm not sure why this and shoveling are my jobs. I should write a post it note about it. I guess that's how we communicate.

~

And here we are, the weeks sliding past. The consequence unstated but becoming clearer and clearer: she will ice me out. Just like the winter. Its below zero days. The frozen helmet of hair. This is her preferred method of punishment: erasure. I am a ghost in my own house. I will leave eventually. I know this already. She'll go on and marry some boring man, live in the suburbs, make a few babies. I know how this story goes.

~

The biggest problem: I'm not one to be silenced. I'm a bit bullheaded. At least, my father always said that.

So, I corner her one afternoon. She's in the kitchen scrawling a post it note to me. She crinkles the note in her palm.

"Well, I guess I can just tell you."

"Tell me what?" I ask.

She clears her throat. "Please dry the counter after washing your dishes."

This is a big step in our relationship. Her saying the thing aloud. I read it as intimacy.

"I guess I can tell you," I begin.

She says, "There's nothing you have to say that I want to hear."

She may be willfully ignorant, but she's not dumb.

"It's perfectly normal," I say. "Beautiful, even."

I feel like the idiot, saying the word *beautiful*.

Carefully, she says, "I don't know what you are talking about."

~

And that's it. That's the consequence. Materially, she increases my rent by $300, knows I can't afford to stay. When I move my last box out, she pretends to be in the bathroom. I knock softly, but it's too soft, even I can barely hear it. I know it's not my job to save everyone. I walk across the living room and close the front door behind me.

Outside, I set my box down on the porch and drag the bins across the driveway one final time. It's not trash day, and the bins are empty, but it feels like something. Like a message. A square yellow note, sticky on one side. A few words jotted across the surface.

Ankit Raj Ojha

ON EDITING

*In Hindi, nouns—even the inanimate—have an assigned gender. "Kavita",
Hindi for poem, is feminine.*

I get this poem every
once in a while who—
as I feast on her full lips—

seduces until she crumbles,
courtesy of her plump belly,
puny pelvis, or feeble legs.

I could suggest edits,
make her desirable
with the poet's consent.

But I hold back, for then
she would be mine too.

And I'd be tempted to keep her.

PHOTOGRAPH BY JEFF BOGLE

ALSO AVAILABLE FROM STANCHION BOOKS

The Woman's Part by Jo Gatford

The House of Skin by Karina Lickorish Quinn

Where We Set Our Easel by Mandira Pattnaik

Irregulars by Kerry Trautman

It Skips A Generation by Alison Lubar

Ghost Mom by T Guzman

The Unaccounted for Circles of Hell by Lynne Schmidt

UNTENABLE MYSTIC CHARM by travis l. tate

Thoughts I Lost in the Laundry by Leia Butler

We Don't Know That This Is Temporary
by Adrienne Marie Barrios

My Dungeon Love Affair by Stephanie Parent

Away From Home Anthology

Ladies, Ladies, Ladies by Kristen Zory King

Mostly Soldiers by Cora Ruskin

The Last Analog Teenagers by Abigail E. Myers

First Kicking, Then Not by Hannah Grieco

Shouldn't We Dance? by Donna-Claire Chesman

An Honor & A Privilege by Lindz McLeod

Learn more at StanchionZine.com